The Great Doughnut Parade

Written and illustrated by

Rebecca Bond

Houghton Mifflin Company • Boston 2007

www.houghtonmifflinbooks.com

The text of this book is set in Garamond.
The illustrations are watercolor and ink.

Library of Congress Cataloging-in-Publication Data

Bond, Rebecca, 1972–
The great doughnut parade / written and illustrated by Rebecca Bond.
p. cm.
Summary: When Billy buys a doughnut and ties it to his belt with
a string while walking down Main Street, he unwittingly sets off a chain of
events that amazes and delights the entire town.
ISBN-13: 978-0-618-77705-1 (hardcover)
ISBN-10: 0-618-77705-9 (hardcover)
[1. Parades—Fiction. 2. Stories in rhyme.] I. Title.

PZ8.3.B599847Gre 2007
[E]—dc22
2006026315

Printed in China
SCP 10 9 8 7 6 5 4 3 2 1

For the BLT bunch,
the lovely crazy lot of you

The great parade began with a doughnut
that Billy had tied to his belt with a string.

The doughnut brought Hen, with a *cluck! cluck! cluck!*
She fancied herself a crumb of this thing.

And then came Cat, all quiet and slinky

and now Big Dog with a bounce like a spring,

together all racing and chasing one doughnut
that Billy had tied to his belt with a string.

Right here and right now, things really got going,
for Daisy in knickers came galloping after.

And that brought the rest of the cast of the play,
all jumbled and tumbled with snorfles of laughter.

And so followed Mabel, their Saturday sitter,
and Adelaide Bead, who'd been doing her hair,

and a whole bunch of runners who saw all this running
and figured the race they were running went there!

Now you can imagine all the confusion
when somewhere on Main Street they picked up a band—

all noisy and joyful and jolly and gleaming,
all beaming with pleasure like this had been planned.

And soon there came others: waiters and diners,
porters with luggage, mailmen with mail,

bricklayers, horn players, painters and masons,
a heavy dirt-digger, a covey of quail.

The firemen came with their firemen's hoses.
The sign painters came with their just-painted signs.

There was a wedding reception with roses.
There was a farmer's full barnyard of swine.

And there were some things you just never saw there—
cloud catchers came with the clouds they had caught.

Citizens came from the pages of history.
Little May Pinker brought things she had thought.

And now the parade—led by one child—
had suddenly swollen to something so wild,

whirling through town so breathlessly fast
that everything shook as the Great Parade passed.

Which would have been fine—
the little town stood.
But for the parade
it didn't look good . . .

Just when their energy couldn't be topped,
right in the front, small Billy—just *stopped*.

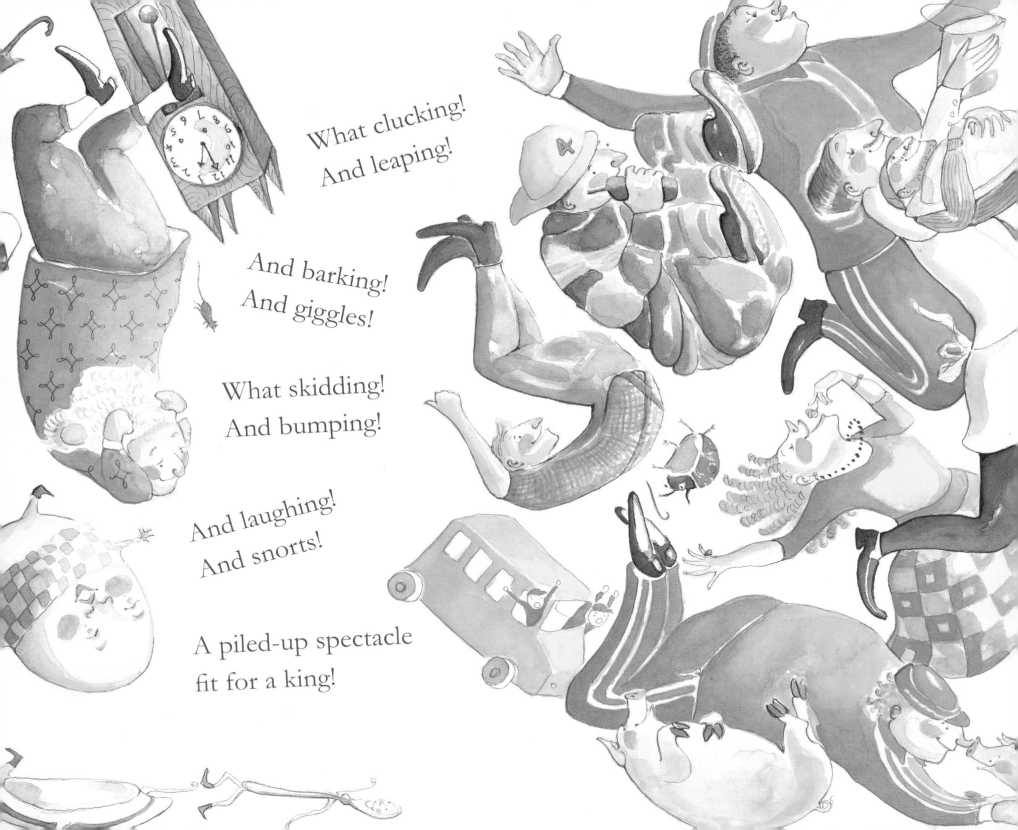

What clucking!
And leaping!

And barking!
And giggles!

What skidding!
And bumping!

And laughing!
And snorts!

A piled-up spectacle
fit for a king!

A splashy display like the bursting of spring!

You never quite think of the marvelous things
that happen when doughnuts are tied up with strings!

And then, with one glance, small Billy departed,
leaving behind this Great Gala he'd started.

He slipped down a path to a spot in the shade,
to a place of pure cool the tallest trees made.

And all afternoon, as the bay bluely gleamed,
this Billy set sail and happily dreamed

while eating a crisp and delicious fried ring—
the doughnut he'd tied to his belt with a string.